Robin Hill School

Halloween
Fun

For JAMB
—M. M.

ALADDIN PAPERBACKS
An imprint of Simon & Schuster Children's Publishing Division
1230 Avenue of the Americas, New York, NY 10020

Designed by Sammy Yuen Jr.
The text of this book was set in Century Schoolbook.
Manufactured in the United States of America
First Aladdin Paperbacks edition August 2008
2 4 6 8 10 9 7 5 3 1
Library of Congress Cataloging-in-Publication Data
McNamara, Margaret.
Halloween fun / by Margaret McNamara ; illustrated by Mike Gordon.
1st Aladdin Paperbacks ed.
p. cm. — (Robin Hill School)
Summary: When first-grader Jamie has a Halloween party that includes a
haunted house, Hannah is nervous to enter until Jamie volunteers to go
too and explain everything to her.
[1. Halloween—Fiction. 2. Haunted houses—Fiction. 3. Fear—Fiction.
4. Friendship—Fiction.]
I. Gordon, Mike, ill. II. Title.
PZ7.M47879343Hac 2008
[E]—dc22
2007046414
ISBN-13: 978-1-4169-3493-6
ISBN-10: 1-4169-3493-6

Halloween Fun

Written by Margaret McNamara
Illustrated by Mike Gordon

Ready-to-Read
Aladdin Paperbacks
New York   London   Toronto   Sydney

Jamie was having a
Halloween party.
All the first graders came.

Katie was a ghost.

Neil, Reza, and Becky
were pirates.

Emma was an elevator.

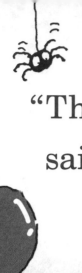

"This is a great party!"
said Ayanna.

"Wait till you see
the fun house!" said Jamie.

"Wow!" said Reza.

"Yo ho!" said the pirates.

"Up, please," said Emma.
They went through the door.

"It is your turn, Hannah," said Jamie.

The fun house
did not look
so fun to Hannah.

It was
dark.

It was creepy.

"I want to go," said Hannah.
"And I also do not."

"Hmm," said Jamie.

"What if we went together?"

Jamie held Hannah's hand.
They went into
the fun house.

Hannah felt a spider web.
"Eek!" she cried.

"The web is fake,"
said Jamie.

"And the spiders
are plastic."

They put their hands
in a bowl of goopy worms.
"Yuck!" said Hannah.

"Those are candy worms
in Jell-O," said Jamie.

"Yum, raspberry,"
said Hannah.

Finally, they saw a WITCH!

"That is my mom!"
said Jamie.
"Hello, Hannah,"
said Jamie's mom.

"Happy Halloween."
She gave Hannah
a bag of candy.

The fun house was done.
"How was it, Hannah?"
asked Jamie.

"Can we go again?"
asked Hannah.

"I did not know
how much fun
I was missing!"